I0566357

Written by: LaShonda C. Henderson

ISBN-13: **978-1-7321319-0-3**
ISBN-10: **1-7321319-0-2**

Published by: Cshantay Publishing

Also by

LaShonda C. Henderson

Love and Other Thoughts

(A book of Poems and Love
Quotes)

Love and Other Thoughts Journal

(A Journal to help Define
individual Love)

*Selah~ The Myth of Love Heart
Changes*

(A Novella)

Capturing Love's Light

(Poems and Prose)

For Love, may we never give up. As
for me, even when I want to, I look at the
LA lights and I am revived.
We deserve love, life says so.

~LaShonda

Contents

Pain and Heartbreak

The hardest part of Heartbreak was removing your clothes from my closet....

The toughest part of Heartbreak was putting your loving cards out of plain sight...

The cleansing part of heartbreak was replacing your memories with the truth...

The reality of heartbreak was loving my heart harder than any pain you caused me...

Welcome heartbreak old friend. When you come around, new love follows and takes me to heights unknown. So instead of heartbreak, we'll rename you "Heart Changes"

I thank you for the Lessons...

For my Community, may we heal

When I was a young girl, bath time was the only peaceful moment I would get.   Growing up with two brothers and a sister, sharing one bathroom meant continuous chaos.

When everyone was distracted and the opportunity reared its head, I would fill the bathtub with water. Not just any water though; I always charged the water with energy; I used those rose scented, water softeners, the kind that fills the room and your soul with scent. Only when my Mom was not home, that way I had no tasks to interrupt the flow.

I would lavish in the silence and relax in the calm of the water, it was peace and I could be anything. The water brought me many imaginings.

I could be a mermaid or a deep-sea diver; whatever I could dream up in the quiet, my favorite thing involved pretending, that through my dainty petite legs, that I was a Water Goddess. I could be in control; my motions could make me powerful, creating tidal waves at will. I would bend my knee to slide up and down the length of the tub, creating fragrant waves of water that moved hurriedly from one side to the next.

If I did it fast enough, spots in the tub, if only for a second, would reveal an empty dry section where you could see the bottom. I would admire the movement but mostly swell with pride at the strength of my legs. I thought how powerful my thighs must be to mimic a natural process that could knock out the strongest of men.

Yet my naivety did not prepare me for the real power these thighs could bring. Opening them to the wrong man can do just as much damage as any tidal wave approaching the shore, knocking many lives off their normal course. Yes, these thighs are powerful; they can destroy many lives if given at the wrong time to the wrong person. I Selah, stand as a witness to the pain thighs can cause in people's lives.

I have seen many thrown off course forever, due to the careless behavior of another person. I want you to understand, I had to become this observer. I am sharing so you gain some understanding, maybe you can even see another way. However, I want to caution you, what I am telling you is not for you to judge the people. It is simply to help you understand that pain changes people. Sometimes forever.

Before I start, let me remind you that our people don't have a soft love. We never really have, as far as the generations I can remember or have heard about. We have a tough love, one just as passionate as we are. It looks different because it must be different. Slavery to freedom, Northerners to Southerners, Love Letters to Fist Fights, our love changed to meet our surroundings.

Oftentimes, it is for the better but most of the time, you'll see the product of the pain sauntering down the sidewalk, spewing its manifestations to every individual who crosses their path.

Yes, pain is an ingrained part of our society, yet, it does not have to end that way. We must discuss it, to address and change, or we can never thrive. I want to take you through a journey of pain. However, do not dare say it was

not love; no matter how disruptive it
sounds.

Come with me.........

Chapter 1
FEAR

Keep walking, no looking back. I know you are tired but you must keep walking, don't give up babies.

I think to myself, "If I don't make it before this sun goes down, we may die." I must make it back to the city before nightfall. I cannot look back. These are the backwoods, we can't see the snakes, if we cannot see the ground. However, I won't say it out loud; I can't tell my kids that, they have been through enough today.

He beat me in front of my kids. What type of man does that? He must be crazy. I must be crazy. My Daddy is going to kill this poor excuse for a man. Walking made my mind drift back to what just happened.

I scream as he hits me again. I do not know how many blows he has given me but I think I am going to pass out. The kids are screaming, their voices keep me conscious. I yell, I think I am yelling, be quiet, I tell myself.

He is dragging me. The brush is ripping my skin the gravel is tearing my flesh. He's going to kill me; I know it, he's going to kill me.

"Baby you ok?" the older woman says with a voice of concern through a rolled down window. Her tone pulls me out of my thoughts. "Yes, I'm alive," why did I say that?

"Do you need a ride?" she urges with her voice.

I was so lost in my thought; I did not even notice her car, much less, hear it slowing down on the roadway. We are walking on this soft shoulder and my mind is a million miles away.

"Yes Ma'am" I say as I lower my head in shame, shrinking inside of myself at the sight she must see. A dirty woman; two small kids and no man walking hurriedly on this countryside; we must be a sight.

"Hop in" she says with a sign of relief in her voice.

I guide the children into the back seat and I sit in the front with her. I sit somberly, and glance back at my son and daughter. They are quiet, not quarreling as they usually do. They are still and quiet.

"Baby, you want to talk about it?" the woman says softly.

"No Ma'am" I utter, "thanks for the ride. You saved us a long walk."

"Where are you headed?"

"Back to the city" I utter. Not ready to decide if I should go to my Father's house or my own.

Luckily, here, when we say "The City" all us country folks on this side of the county know what we mean. The city is where all the houses and commerce reside. I tell her, the city, so she understands that I just want to be where human life is after this day I have had.

She smiles and begins to drive her comfortable safe automobile.

The daylight is beginning to break the light from the sky; it is acting, as I feel right now inside, down. The sun is setting and my hopes of me and my man ever getting back together are going down too. He tried to kill me. Not just kill me; he tried to kill me in front of my kids in an isolated spot where no one would find me. How did we get to that place?

All I did was ask him where he was. All I did was ask him, why Lucy felt like she could grin at me the way she did. I should be able to ask my husband that! I mean what is wrong with that? I am his wife; I am entitled to ask questions.

"Baby you sure you don't want to talk about it?" She breaks the conversation in my head.

I look at the backseat, and see my children sleeping. I burst into tears. I cannot help myself.

The woman pulls the car over to the side of the road. She reaches for me, and I shrink back.

"Aww Honey, I'm not here to harm you. I would never harm you" She coaxes.

Tears running down my face, dirt coating my hair, my skin bleeding from being drug along the coarse pavement, I melt into the seat a little.

"She reaches for my hand and strokes it softly. "Baby, I have seen many things in this life, but I haven't ever seen a man change unless he wanted to. A man did this to you didn't he."

I shook my head, still gasping for air while the tears fought for space on my cheeks.

"You ain't got to tell me, they think they own us." She sounded very haughty and angry.

"No, I made him do this" I stated firmly.

Looking at me all bewildered and confused. She took a deep breath. I could tell she was choosing her words carefully.

"You ain't did nothing." She said through clenched teeth, "that made you deserve THIS."

She points to me.

"Look at yourself", she reaches over, planting her hand on the roof of my side of the car, just above the windshield and thrust down. Still a little shaken from the events of the day, I bow my head.

"Look", she huffs.

Holding my head up, I notice a visor, the type with lights and a mirror, shining in front of me.

"You take a good look at your face" She says to me, sounding angry.

I hold my head up and see swollen eyes. The eyelids were not a normal pecan color of skin; instead, they displayed ones that were rapidly turning dark, like rotten meat. The complete left side of the face was large and protruding from its normal shape. Lips swollen, corners filled with dried blood, having burst open from the pressure of a fist.

My beautiful face lay open, broken, pride scattered all over it like the remains of a battlefield. Like a war, I had lost terribly. No wonder my kids were crying so loudly. No wonder I felt so lost and outside of myself. He had beaten who I was away. My face was the proof of it. "That is not me", I thought.

Then suddenly, as I stared intently, those dark puffs began to ooze water, which turned into streaks of mud and blood. A mixture; of muck, poured down that girl's face, the one in the mirror.

This cannot be real, that girl looks unloved and a horrid mess. That is not me. I reach up to my face, and that girl in the mirror echoes the same movement, I touched my eyes and winced from the pain, I stroked what could not be my cheek and felt tingles of pressure and pain.

My husband did this to that girl in the mirror. He did this to ME, his wife. All I did was ask a question.

Tears began rising from what felt like my stomach. I could feel; water, pain, and energy coming up from the bottom of my body, out through these meat bags of eyes. He beat who I was away.

"You still ain't gone say nothing." She hissed.

"No Ma'am," I say. Still trying to process how that girl, that battered girl in THAT mirror in front of me could be the strong Woman that I am.

Ain't no way that's me.

Suddenly she slid over and hugged me. She grabbed me gently and hugged my doubt away.

That was I. That girl in the mirror is me. I am hurt. My face hurts and my pride is hurt. This stranger is holding me, hugging me as my husband's arms were supposed to do when I asked him those questions. This stranger is providing me comfort as I sit in her space, broken physically and mentally. I am not a strong woman. I am that girl in the mirror. That poor broken girl. Poor me.

I pull back from her.

She looks at me knowingly and slides back to her side of the car back under the steering wheel. She hands me some tissue from a box on the floor and I mutter, "thank you" ...between my gasps for air.

It hurts to breathe.

I glance in the mirror one more time. Looking closer at the damage, I could see my kids sound asleep in the back. I flip the mirror up and turn my head, to look at the setting sky, as she slowly pulls the car back on the road. Yes. He did this to me.

She breaks the monotony of the engine sound, bouncing through the car.

"Honey, I'm not going to tell you what to do with your life. But do you want to die?"

I swallow hard. I want to scream, I am already dead, look at me. My face, who I was, what I looked like is dead. My nose must be broken; my forehead filled with pain. The parts that make me, who I am, ARE already dead.

However, I mutter, "No Ma'am".

Then, I am going to tell you some hard truth. Baby, I can see you have a ring on. I know that you are married and that you belong to him. Never the less, there ain't no shame in going back to your Daddy girl. You ain't got to lie and tell me that this is his first time; he's put his hands on you. Because baby where I just picked you up from, ain't nothing out here but crops and livestock.

"You all got farming plots out this way", she asked me; I could feel her looking over at me for an answer.

"No Ma'am," I said quietly.

I am going to tell you the truth, ask your Momma if you don't believe me.

"My Momma is dead," I interrupted.

"I'm sorry to hear that she said solemnly, changing her tone."

Baby, he did not bring you all the way out here with your kids to pick no crops. You ain't out here to feed no livestock.   Were   you   headed

somewhere?

"No Ma'am," I shook my head.

"He brought you out here to

harm you. He wanted to hurt you, I

cannot say what made him do it, now I

don't know your situation, but I can say

he has proven you are in danger."

I shifted in my seat and looked at

her. She had to be at least 60, this

woman is my elder and here she is

telling me that MY husband wanted to

harm ME.

"Are you saying that he?"

…I'm angry now…

"You do not know my husband, he chose me. He married ME, he loves ME."

The sound of movement in the back makes me stop speaking. I turn my head and see my son shifting in the seat, his eyes still closed.

Honey, ain't no love on your face. Did you see your face baby? That is all rage, and anger. I know it ain't my business.   You are a woman, so your

pain is MY pain. Baby, he hurt us.

I looked over, and noticed the

tears streaming down her face.

What does she mean us? I'm the

one sitting here with my face all

distorted and body bruised, I'm the one

whose husband just violated me

because of stupid ass Lucy. There ain't

no us. This woman is crazy.

I turn my head towards the

window.

We make it towards the city and I decided. I was going home; back to my husband.

I break the silence by giving her the directions, telling her where to turn to get to my house.

She never said another word, after her tears started falling. She just drove.

We pull up to our house and my husband is standing outside smoking a cigarette. The woman stops the car. I get out and open the door; as I do, my husband walks towards the car.

"The kids are in the back," I say softly, but respectfully through my swollen lips.

He speaks to the woman. "Thank you for bringing them home Ma'am." Then he slides the kids out, one after the other, into his strong arms, the proof of their strength hidden all over my body, but displayed well on my face.

As I stand there, looking at his gentleness with the kids. He walks around to the driver's side of the car.

"Can I give you some gas money," he says to the woman.

Tears running down her face, she manages the words, "No that's ok" then easily, "I d-o n-o-t n-e-e-d a-n-y," oozes out of her mouth contempt vibrating into every syllable that she uttered.

He steps away from the car, looking defeated with the kids in his arms.

She pulls away.

He steps over to me, looking angry. "Did you tell her our business?" I walk slowly back into our house, holding the door open for him.

I will keep my mouth closed tonight.

Today taught me that I should keep it

closed tonight.

Chapter 2
Reality

He tried to kill us.

Then I had to walk into school as if nothing happened. I do not even get to cry. I get to put on the brave face of, "At least I am here" and go on with life. That is what Momma said this morning. "At least we are alive."

I do not get to mourn for any part of me that dies every time the crazy begins to escalate. I do not get to cry and be comforted because the world definitely does not care. The world does not want to hear any sorrow from me. I am just a little girl. My wants fail to matter. If they did, that woman in that car would not have brought us back to that house; she would have taken us somewhere safe. Somewhere normal, where parents are not allowed to try and kill each other in front of their kids.

This world does NOT care.

Nobody cares about the wants of a child. Therefore, I sit here quietly in this classroom looking down at my class work. This world doesn't care. So, why should I?

When I grow up; ain't nobody ever going to be able to hurt me. I am going to marry the strongest man I can find. One who would beat Daddy up if he ever tried to hurt me like he does Momma. He is going to protect me. Unlike all these people in this, mean world.

"Come here," my teacher yells out. Do you want me to call your Momma?

"No Ma'am," I utter.

Well stop staring into space and move your pencil. Do your work young lady.

"Yes Ma'am," I utter.

As I shuffle back to my desk, I hear giggles in the classroom.

Nope, this world definitely doesn't care about a little girl like me. I begin to do my work silently.

Chapter 3
The Truth

I lay still in my bed.

They are watching me; waiting for me to break down. I see it in their smirks when I cross over into their realm. That is why I hate to dream, I will not sleep willingly, and I wait until my body forces it. I feel like the ancestors are waiting for me to crack.

They must whisper, "This is a strong one, we made her strong," as I rise to meet every challenge this life throws at me.

But, I am not.

I am a ticking time bomb waiting for the reason to act out on the pain that everyone heaped upon me. A childhood filled with violence; in my house, in my neighbor's houses, made me this way.

They say people like me turn to drugs and alcohol to release the pain, but not me. I want to face it head-on. I want to see the result of the horror this community caused me. They broke me before any other race or societal group could. Do not talk to me about any oppressor outside of us.

No one could ever break me, because my family did that, they broke me before I could ever have a chance in the world...my family did that. They took away my ability to love and have a normal relationship. THEY DID THIS TO ME. Nope do not tell me about an oppressor other than the people who I watched, hold me down physically and mentally.

No child should ever have to sit and wonder, is this the day we die? Is this the day that he decides to kill us?

The thoughts race in my mind as I lay in this bed. It always comes back to me during the darkness of the night. That day is stuck on repeat in my head. Who could ever forget the day the police came and took your Daddy? No one could forget about the day their Daddy went to jail.

She egged him on, I heard her shouting, "oh you're not a man you'll never do it. You're too weak to hurt anything."

I stood there, everything inside of me was screaming then; "he is already doing it Momma. He is hurting us every single day. Killing everything, I could ever want to be."

Maybe he heard it in my head shouting to his soul, I do not know. All I know is that right then, he did it. He killed her.

He killed my Momma.

All I could do was grab my brother's hand and sit there. Waiting for the only time when the world cared, when somebody died, to show up and act concerned.

He killed my Momma.

I sit here with my mind in the clouds reliving how this world doesn't care about me. How I watched, how no one saved my Momma. The community watched him kill her and the spirits of both her children.

I blame them for my brother being locked up now; he is an outcome, the residual pain. He is just like his Daddy, violent as hell.

My brother may have loved my Momma, but he never loved any women he lay with. He didn't love anybody. So, I can't say I was surprised when he went to jail like Daddy. What else was he supposed to do?

Violence in our house, and the community reinforced his behavior through every brawl. They chanted and high fived him for winning. He had to prove he was tough. He had to show them he wasn't no punk. Nobody respects a punk.

I sit here watching the stars, wondering. How do we get past this pain and heartbreak?

The ancestors must be watching and be very concerned, because no one in this world cares. They must be smirking, saying, "this one we made her strong."

But I am not.

I lay down to sleep and escape all chaos this world brings. The community killed me before I had a chance.

"This world doesn't care," I thought as I unwillingly closed my eyes from all this grief, this sorrow, this Pain.

Loving in Babylon's Garden

You see…
Here in Babylon
They teach you to go for yours
Without regard to feelings, consequences or
future
They teach the NOW
But
This life isn't just about you

Here in Babylon
They want you to isolate yourself
Without regard to patterns, stigmas or
legacy
But generations are watching

Here in Babylon
They want you to forget love
Without regard to tenderness, affection or
concern
They teach
Life doesn't require it
But hearts don't beat without it
You see
They want you distracted so you cannot
reach the garden
Disappoint them, submit to your higher
self, serve one another…
Enter the Garden of Eden
The gate is always open
For Love

Chapter 1

I want you to know, I tried. Not the "College Try", but a consistent, intense, give it my all try. But in Babylon they don't want love, they want status, they want accolades, they want to win, by any means necessary.

I'm just a woman. ONE woman, who wanted to give love a chance. What is one woman against a million who just want to be seen? Babylon means chaos. Some call it a specific place, a city, which was the birthplace of confusion and division; it does not really matter in which city I am.

For I am in THIS Century and THIS time in history, requires no specific location, it is a widespread mass of disarray, mass division and most of all, mass disruption of the spirit.

The longer you are in a place, the more likely you are to adopt the ways of the majority. It doesn't even happen all at once, it happens subtly. First you sound like them, then you walk like them, next thing you know, you have picked up the behaviors of those native to the area.

It is human nature. We want to conform.

But should we? There are definitely times we should, because we need the ability to "blend in" for progress. But what about those other times? You know, when we need to stand alone?

I took an executive public speaking class many moons ago. They had many confidence building exercises, one of the exercises was called, "Entering a Room". The participants were simply asked to walk in a room, and then receive feedback from classmates about the type of energy you project.

There were only twelve participants other than me, but watching each person walk in; I mean, being intentionally aware; of their full body, clothing and stride, taught us all something. Where you are from, whom you hang around and your speech style, all put you in a category; it is a quick boil down glimpse of how you are expected to behave. But walking into a room, no words are spoken, you are just a human entering a space and though you can walk like everyone else in the area, you can mimic the mannerisms; the emotions that enter with you, are another thing.

It was easy to tell who was sure of themselves, who was nervous and who didn't want to be there. Even when they KNEW, we were watching, they were AWARE of the judgment; emotions still came pouring out as they walked into the door.

It is like that being in Babylon, everyone is always watching and no one is able to hide from the witnesses, and we see FEAR.

Chapter 2
No Regrets

They keep asking me why I won't settle
down...

I say...Dust Settles
Noise settles
A child settles
A storm settles
Because they have too, I don't...

They keep asking, with their sad faces,
heavy hearts after another episode of, "As
the tears roll."

They ask politely, ring finger shining.

Here in Babylon, settling means lying down
and you can't see the enemy coming if you
are prostrated and comfortable. Ask
Delilah, Mary, or your beloved Pop Star of
the Moment.

They want me to settle, but I want to
STAND

Here in Babylon, they want me to

get married. Me!!!! (Bends over in cackling

laughter), but I'm not the marrying type. I see all of these women walking around here pretending to be happy. Yea, I said it. They PRETEND to be happy. Who can be happy when your "Man" can't be controlled? I mean he shows up for family functions, gives you holiday time then lays his head on YOUR bed after a long day of chasing after me and anyone else with a skirt.

Nope, not I, I don't want it.

I don't intend to settle. I don't think this Century understands or can even grasp what GOD meant by marriage.

Stop laughing Selah, I believe in GOD.

I'm not one of those go to Church types, but I believe. I get, order must exist, that something out there created us to do "good", whatever that means.

I see that look of confusion on your face; I'll bet you are wondering how I can believe in the Creator but not believe in Marriage.

You've got me all wrong. I said, "I" am not the marrying "TYPE". I'm not talking about how it was created in the beginning. I'm talking about the ownership; that I've got papers on you, type here in Babylon.

I mean, read the bible and even in THAT text there is some confusion about what marriage means. Going by the Old Testament, you'll find the first instructions from GOD; "man and woman will become one flesh" it is in the book Genesis 2:24 I think. Heck, you will even find a Proverb, somewhere in 18, around verse 22, insinuating, and "It is good for man to find a wife".

But, if you've read the whole thing, that thousand plus page book, you'll see in the New Testament, Peter instructs to the church that a woman is the, "weaker vessel". How did we go from being, "one flesh", to a "weaker vessel"? I don't get it.

But THAT is exactly what they think here in Babylon; Wives are fragile and weak. That makes less sense than the man in the moon.

I see you shaking your head, I don't know if you agree are disagree.

But tell me, I'm going to lean in close so I can hear this answer, when DID WE BECOME WEAK? Where do you see these weak women? I mean babies come through us, and history tells that we are KNOWN for hearing the voice of the beyond. Religious or not, we act as the channel for whatever is out there, look at the epic poems and verses, ALL of the seers were women. They carried the divine word. They came to US for direction.

HERE in Babylon, Men drive the car. They are the ones who run this whole world! If they run this world, that means they think they run my body. But Selah, I'm going to lean back and tell you the cool truth and I'm going to cross my arms and legs, because that is exactly what I do to these men. Close them away from my heart and my gifted "future/legacy" canal.

They are at war with WOMANHOOD. They hate who we are and the life we bring forth, even if life is a mirror of their self. They want me to lay down and receive the poison they wrap in a pretty box, gifted with ribbons and sparkles; that they didn't even make! I'm no dummy.

Even that bible, the one they use as a weapon against my womanhood, says, "Wisdom is the principle thing and with wisdom get understanding". Lady, I understand! I know, I hear daily, HERE in Babylon we are at WAR!

So, no I don't want to get married, because I don't sleep with the enemy; I can see the concern in your eyes. I'm no fool; I know that there are some men who don't think like that. But they don't have as loud a voice. They are isolated, with soft voices and are often labeled as weak and fragile; by other men and EVEN some women, can you imagine some of "US", see them as less than men. Let me tell you...

Chapter 3

And I've heard...
In Babylon's Garden,
There are pockets of bliss.
Spots where the flowers were always in
bloom.
But those spots are private...those who
Visit it on the regular don't share its
location.
It is unbound by rules, words or actions.
That part of the GARDEN is blessed and
not everyone is allowed to live or even visit
I've heard...
But I believe them
They have a peace about them
Not ALL of the plants in Babylon's Garden
are poison
But not everyone knows that...

Can you imagine Selah? Can you

envision what's it like being with a man that

people, male and female called weak? We

are at war; against common sense and good

intentions. I'll tell you, they don't want anything righteous.   They want what Babylon told them they should have. They want someone who owns them and stifles their connection to the great IAM.

It is a scheme Selah.

The old bait and switch; and people are falling for it. Women will tell you, I don't want a piece of a man, I want a whole one.

But WHAT IS a whole one? The most they can tell you is a character; one like that digital Chatter Box, programs them to   want.   That   chatterbox,   TV/ programming, or whatever you want to label it, is a hostile takeover, a poor excuse of instruction. They do it on purpose; I mean, distract people from the real.

But, I've had one of those men and I'll tell you, the wholeness they try to feed you and my wholeness is NOT the same thing.

Humph

It is not.

I'm not a person who will tell you something I didn't try. I tried to love the men Babylon cranked out. I really did.

I shut my mouth, looked pretty and laughed at the jokes. I became one of these robots you see running around this chaos, you know dressed alike, smiling alike, hair alike, but as I told you before, my emotions could never be like them. I would act like them, but I couldn't be them. Therefore, I would publicly do what was required of me. Conform. But when I was alone with the men, I'd be me.

I'd seduce the "original man" out of him. No, I'm not talking about sex; I'm talking about, what was given to him in the beginning. My home, my space was the sanctuary. The right scents, the right noise level, the perfect place to commune with the Most HIGH. In my space, there is no room for poison.

It is peace within these walls. They'd find me when they grew tired of the nonsense; of the made-up story this world gave them. I would let the man I loved not those I liked, lie in my bosom. I would comfort his senses from this chaos. The ones I liked, I listened like a dutiful sister or cousin. They'd take from me. But, I'd give freely.

They'd bask in the peace, mellow in the scents and splay their cares before the altar that was my heart.

I tried to heal them. I really did. You see, chaos is like a sickness that rides you and no medicine can cure you of it. It was overwhelming.

Let me be silent for a minute, I don't want to cry before you, you might think I'm weak or something and you'd miss my

message. Just let me take a deep breath.

So many times I almost lost myself.

But I never lost the softness.

Chapter 4

And you know...
Loving him was like, being rescued
Not one of those happy ending types
though.
It was like I was one of those victims, one
whose heart stopped beating.
And when your heart stops, you need extra
oxygen to breathe, so he gave me his breath,
his kiss of life
But that wasn't the problem
You see, that breath brought my mind back
to life, but it was my heart that needed the
help
And He tried to help me, but being
uncertified
He hurt me, more than I already was...
But he only cracked a rib, I'm still alive you
see.
So, I ask...did he save Me?
I'm breathing, but I'm broken...
Should I be grateful or mad
Hell, I don't know.
But I'll tell you something...I'M HERE to tell
you this story.
Love ain't easy...but I know I don't have to
tell you THAT

Selah, what I will tell you is this…

He was the man of my dreams literally; everything that I prayed for in essence, without words, in that spiritual realm.

I keep telling you, I'm not one of the ones from Babylon; I didn't have a list or quota to meet. I wasn't asking for a thing, but the ability to help me reach the Most High.

He was ALL THAT, standing before my face, like a trinket uncovered by one of those Archeologists you see on TV, unveiling a new find. No, I'm not talking about his physical; I'm speaking more on connection level.

Don't look at me like that; I know what you're thinking. But I'm not talking about a sexual thing. Don't be fooled by what they tell you in these streets, a man has NO control over your orgasm. YOU do! So, uh-uh oh no, I'm not talking about that.

If you knew how to tap into your own sexual power, no man could ever disappoint you and you wouldn't think that they held that type of power. You've probably forgotten about your power, as most of these women do. I can tell, by that stunned look and that mouth wide open, but I am off track here, back to him.

He had this way about him. Like God could speak through him. I really believe the MOST HIGH did. But like any prophet, he ran from his calling. I wish I had paid attention to that fact. You see, if a Man will run from GOD he'll run from you too. I should have been the one running if you ask me. But, he really could heal your spirit with a hug. I know, because that is how he got me.

I was having a bad year, ok couple of years and there he was, arms all open. I walked into them without hesitation, not my usual behavior, because I have this thing about touch.

Before that hug, I was still a little girl; a tiny little frail thing, in a grown woman's body. I mean, that little girl in me was broken from inappropriate touches, harsh words and negligent behavior from adults in my childhood; and I was supposed to be this grown woman, poised and normal. However, I was not, looking at me there was no sign; you would think, I had it all together.

But, I was still shattered inside, cringing from touch, you could see my ribs, I was starving from lack of real connection. I was taxed, out here healing men who didn't want to give me shield nor armor in return.

I thought he was different because the MOST HIGH dwelled with him. So, I gave into this Man. I opened every single facet of my Womanhood to him. My spiritual and my physical, I showed him my Divine Feminine, and he violated me. Yea he hugged me, opening that spiritual realm for me, but he also tortured the physical mind that was me, and I walked away more broken than I was when he met me. I mean it is easy to live in Babylon pretending. You get your hair and nails done, throw on some name brand clothes, and walk with purpose in those shoes with color on the bottom, all the while clutching your "BAG" for dear life.

I looked good. But HE VIOLATED ME, not that outside me they were used to seeing, I'm talking that Divine Feminine me.

Chapter 5

And I want you to be silent...
Just as silent, as you were
When you watched him
Murder her character, her spirit...her legacy
And I want you to be silent...
But gleeful
Like you were when he was getting over
You know high fives
Toasts to the pimp life
Noisy with celebratory gulps
And I want you to be silent...
Like you can hear a pin drop
You know, like it was when you saw him
hugged up with someone who wasn't her
Be silent
No inbox telling lies about how he loves her
He's just a man
No phone calls talking about chill out
You're taking it too far
No emails about how he's hurting
While her wounds are still visibly bleeding
No texts about his state of mind
You watched her lose her a long time ago
I want you to do what we do here in
Babylon, shut the f up...when we attack our
GREAT FEMININE.
When we defile her temples.

When we spray paint her walls with
ANOTHER CASUALTY.
Do what we do here, Celebrate a new thing
to gossip about.
And I want you to be silent
Look, there she goes...
She left...
Just as silently as she walked in...
shhhhh
Here in Babylon...we don't have a heart
condition...we have a rampant disease...

Let me tell you how he violated me.

Man....Selah, heart disease is highly

contagious. There is no pill that can relieve

the suffering it causes.

Back in the day women were treated

with Divinity.   People understood that

women are blessed, so they placed you on a

pedestal not to be touched with filthy hand

or   vicious   intentions.   Maybe   I'm

romanticizing it, but I don't know of a time, except slavery where women were treated so poorly. Maybe, that is where it started; this disease I mean, because before now, they were on a completely different level. Women were revered; some women were even required to be virgins their whole lives. But they had a system in place.

In this time period, right now, in this Babylon, there is no pedestal. There are no Fathers to protect your virginity, no Uncles to avenge if you are wronged, no brothers who were connected to your plight. Everyone was out for self. The men, who would have stood up for you back then, hand you over here.

Stop Crying Selah.

It is just truth. Heart disease makes people do the strangest things. But, listen my love, I did this to myself.

I chose him by myself. I was naked, unprotected spiritually and physically. I should have sought guidance, but that is against the "Feminine Code", it says I'm supposed to be powerful and righteous by birth. But I wasn't. I was vulnerable here, with no one to help save me from myself.

I opened my Divinity and he wrecked my Temple. He brought chaos, the heart disease with him. The crazy part is, they helped him. Other women helped him hurt me; they run in packs here in Babylon.

No one does a thing alone, except the outsiders. The Outsiders don't know better, we weren't raised here, but these natives, they are equipped and they have a system. They jump you together, cracking ribs, stealing your breath, pounding your ideas into the ground; while the men cheer. Your life is a coliseum and they are sitting in the stands cheering for the lion, which is HIM, to devour you.

The first symptom of heart disease is groupthink. It begins as a trickle and spreads until it ruptures the heart until it just stops beating. But before it ruptures, you must understand the second symptom, which is that blank stare they have. It comes from the blood doing its job in their body. You see blood is made mostly of water, but it also carries oxygen and when the brain can't get oxygen, it makes a corpse out of you. They are walking corpses and they'll kill you for simply being alive.

What made it harder for me is that I saw the Most High riding him.

What do I mean?

I could see generations through his eyes, I could see peace in his core, and I smelled the Garden coming through his pores. He helped me reach it on many occasions, and then he would punish me through some mundane action, for opening it up in him, for helping him see the light of peace. He thought he didn't deserve peace; so he would punish me. How? He knew my ego; he would say mean things or do things he knew would hurt my pride. It seemed he wanted to beat the light out of my head, but I wanted to help him walk in the Garden every day. I wanted to help relieve him, you know, revive his heart.

I told you before, I'm a healer, I wanted him to stand straight without the disease trampling his being; corpses are stiff and coarse. I wanted him to heal, not so I could have him, but so he could be free from that little boy of his past like I was set free from that fragile girl. But like I told you he fought me.

He preferred the fight and he did not care if he had to be wicked, as long as it caused pain!

I'm not just saying this because I felt hurt, I told you the truth. I had to leave him because like a typical Babylonian, he loved Money way more than he could have ever loved me or himself.

Chapter 6

When I was young...
I dated a dude so deep in the game, he lost
his emotions...
So deep in the money
IT became his GOD...
He would buy me anything
but he never gave me anything of value...
He owned me like property
I gave him the leaseeventually, he got 1 case
3 charges...40 years concurrently
When I was young...
I stood by him
I visited him
I waited
While we were young
He changed before my eyes
He had to face himself
He found GOD within
He spoke to the GOD in me
He gave me back my lease
He released me
When I was young
He saved me
From his old life
When I was young
GOD set me free
Him letting me go...now THAT is Loyalty

He isn't the first man, heck person, who loved money Selah. I have met men who did all kinds of sketchy things to obtain a dollar. However, he was the first man who had the MOST HIGH on his back that loved it so much. Now, I know you are thinking; what about these Preachers, Reverends, and Pastors, but I will tell you it is not the same. Anyone can say the GOD called them, but the ones who were really called are AFRAID.

They are fearful.

He was scared, but that does NOT excuse his wickedness. He wanted to destroy me, just for turning his face to the light. I didn't approach him. He approached me. I just watched him, like you do. Learning who he was and trying to be understanding of why he wouldn't let GOD through. He hated me for that. Not in those individual moments where we were helping one another dwell in the Garden. But in those big ones where I was reminding him of his higher calling. He might as well have drug me through the streets by my hair like my Dad did to my Mom that one time, and paraded me to the center of Babylon then stamped my head with the word "WHORE" because that is how I felt.

He imprisoned me, for their Money, what they deemed cash flow!

Locked me up behind their expectations and slammed the door on my life. Every time I praised him, he'd smear my name through the mouth of the crowd. He'd lay down with another woman, or parade her on his arm. I did not respond to those types of attacks, it is minuscule to me. So he'd kiss them and hug them in front of me. Kiss them, with the same mouth that produces blessings! Hug them with the arms that opened the gates to the Garden, I'd shout internally, "who does he think he his?" I tell you it was pure wickedness! He'd do it until I was ready to tear the streets up with my bare hands. Then he'd see me rage and feel remorseful.

He'd feel sorry and blame an outside force for the problem. But really it was him. He knew it and sometimes, he'd release me;

just let me go and I'd flee with my pride in shambles, feeling raw and raped. But I'd turn inward Selah.

I wouldn't let the disease get in.

I'd pray to the MOST HIGH, to right my heart and not let the blood stop flowing oxygen to my brain, I'd ask for permission to breathe; to not become a corpse like them, and the Most High would make him release me momentarily. Because we know our troubles are our own, God doesn't play favorites.

Those were the hardest moments Selah. I'd feel as though I had gone insane. Every part of me, muscles and thoughts would freeze up. Feeling sore, yet numb; no that is not it, everything would feel heavy. My thoughts, the light, the currency of life…love, would feel heavy. It was in those times that I wanted to escape.

Chapter 7

And I wanted to scream at her
so she'd hear me
I wanted it to stop
Because, she'd be free of him, then he'd
meander right back into her life,
simply to love on her for a minute
One single minute
my mouth would be wide open as she
responded to him...
she'd forget
all the hours she spent healing
from the last episode
I wanted to scream at her...
But love made her deaf.
Maybe I should have learned sign
language...

You know Selah, when you enter the

Garden you always want to return! It is

paradise and you can't ever forget what it

feels like. No matter how wicked he was to

me, I was like a little kid, running to the

gates to greet him. Every time he'd return,

it hurt a little more. I just wanted, to not hurt anymore, but I also wanted to heal him. I wanted us both to heal, but my focus was mostly him, it seemed he needed it more.

It was hard.

I mean when you are dealing with the MOST HIGH, how do you turn your back? There was no way out that I could see, except for separating the two. I had to release my image of him and the spirit that rode him.

Don't look at me all crazy, I am not talking about no voodoo or hoodoo or whatever they call it. I'm talking about shaking him off of me. I could only try to do it the way I knew how, using my womanly love, kisses, love and physical release, as only we can do.

I prayed so hard. Looking into the proverbs and saying the words of peace before I saw him. Then I would call him over.

I always kissed him one last time before I began, then I would make love to him in my way. I seduced his spirit and loved his physical then whispered the words of release to his soul. It was nothing complex. It was just a simple request, "let me go". He responded back with "NO", and he meant it. It didn't work, he didn't want it to.

What do I mean he didn't want it to?

Selah, I am no fool.   Men are stronger than women physically, and EVERY woman knows that if you release a man in the wrong way, it can cost your life! This is no metaphor, they will kill you.   He was stronger than me and I would go days, ignoring him; being completely silent. Not uttering one word of praise or upliftment. I refused to talk to him or his spirit.

But, I'd break. It was like he had a hold on me. I would wake up in the middle of the night, his face before my eyes. His scent on my pillow, his love floating in those little white spaces, you know, the ones you see when you close your eyes? I would wake like a drug addict! Saying his name into the night and whispering, "I love you into the space" like he could hear me.

I would be dying to talk to him, just to, hear his voice. I felt like I needed him, as he said he needed me. When we got back together, we would go right back into the cycle of things. Except now, it was even more hostile, because he knew I wanted to let him go.

We were like wild animals hunting one another. Selah, I had to stop, I wanted to.

Chapter 8

Love is a jungle But even in a jungle...
There are beasts, birds and snakes
And THOSE "animals", they are pacing
waiting for an opening
You see...
Love is a jungle
But even in a jungle...
There is not much penetration of light, it is
much too dense
You have to use your own light
But, the "animals" oh they see you
The gentle "creatures"...they wait
Because they are being hunted too
Love is a jungle
But If you forget where the switch to your
light is...
Look for the Light out THERE
Turn towards the Light, so you can see my
dear
Because in the Light..you can see, if it is an
"animal" or a "creature" you are dealing
with...
Love is a jungle
But even in a jungle...
There is ALWAYS a path to civilization
Sometimes that path is BABYLON
But...sometimes...the path leads to EDEN

Orient yourself...then step on your path
wisely...
But whatever you do...DON'T lay down
with the ANIMALS no matter what they
say...
Because when you do, they will surely
devour you...

Selah, I wish we could have stopped. I knew we were playing a dangerous game. That one of us would be so hurt, that there would be no coming back. But neither of us could stop. Some days he was the animal, being vicious and mean. Some days he was the creature, being gentle and kind. I didn't know what I would get each day.

It was maddening!

It was the foundation for insanity I tell you. I'm strong though. I watched his moves. I watched the things he stayed away from and the things that made his heart leap with joy. I watched it all. You see, if you want to learn what moves a man, watch him with no judgment. Just watch.

He was an intense man. The women, the partying, the strolls through his "jungle" were just an act. He never even liked those things. Because when no one was looking, he looked so sad, so lost, so forlorn; then it hit me. He wasn't trying to hurt me. He was trying to toughen me up. He knew what it felt like to be lost in this jungle. He knew those women didn't love him.   He knew those people didn't love him.   He was doing exactly what I was. God was riding his spirit and he was obeying.   Turning people to the light how they needed it. While it may have felt like it was a violation to me. It was his calling.

He was refusing to release me because I was the thing he needed.   The acceptance, the understanding he had been searching for. I was like him, he was like me. We were both lightworkers.

You don't know what a lightworker is? Selah, you are one. It is a person whose only job in this world is to turn mankind back to structure, honor, to themselves; their spiritual selves.   This world, this jungle is full of distractions. A lightworker is tasked with returning a person's spirit back to the Most High. We are what we worship. Here in Babylon, people worship THINGS. Turning their hearts back towards the internal light stream is what they do.

He was that. Like all lightworkers it is exhausting work. Some have breakdowns and turn to alcohol or drugs or sex. But the thing they never do is stop turning people towards the light.

It is a heavy task, and sometimes we get caught up. Sometimes we become acclimated to Babylon and before long, even lightworkers, cannot release themselves from the chaos. That is why only the Most High could make him release me in moments when it got too heavy for MY heart. That is why he never wanted to release me for the long run. He needed me to refuel. I can't lie Selah, I needed him too.

Chapter 9

I use to spend MY days
Watching out for women
Who came at my man...
I was trying to keep him acting "right".
Now I spend my days watching my heart,
trying to keep it "feeling" right!
The only disrespect I look for NOW can be
found solely in my actions towards my
spirit

Selah, dry your face girl.

This is just life. No need for the tears! Here in Babylon, they will attack you for that.

So, can you understand? Do you get why I would not marry here? Only that man was allowed to get close to my spirit. I don't want anyone else but him. But not to own him, I just want him, to help me refuel from time to time.

So no, I never released him. He never released me. But I am NOT married. I'm doing my work. Standing tall here in Babylon trying to survive! I'm trying to keep from becoming a corpse while dwelling in EDEN from time to time with HIM.

You see Selah; nothing here, in Babylon, is as it appears. I did stop the pain. I exited his path. I left his jungle. I live in my own space, away from his work. I let him do his job. I don't look for reasons to be mad anymore.

I let him be.

Selah, isn't that what we really want? I mean, we all just want to... just BE.

I will be careful.

I will not allow anyone else, on accident or purpose, to dwell in our Garden.   It belongs to just us two. Whatever he does in Babylon belongs to him and The Most High who rides and guides him.

But as for me; I'm no fool.

I belong to me.   I do my work without exposing myself to the violence he puts himself in. I am a lightworker. I am the MYTH of LOVE. But him, I truly LOVE.

Thank you for listening Selah.

Choices

Believe me, I've tasted bad love
His was different, but it definitely wasn't
bad
I know, because it did something to me
And there wasn't a thing "Bad" about the
outcome
His love found me
That deep down ME
And turned me out
No, it wasn't bad
It was that
Revolutionary
Type of love
And I chose it….

Chapter 1

Choices?   What the hell do they know about choices? I'm just a person, not a GOD, I know my limitations! I belong to the ones who created everything. I'm just an observer in my life, watching the path change based on where fate said it should go.   Choice?   I direct nothing, I know nothing, I'm a victim! A damn victim and no I did NOT choose that!   Because if I could, who would choose a life like mine? You tell me who.

Naw, do not give me that choices bull, you tell me how…you explain how to avoid pitfalls on this path called "MY LIFE". Just tell me how I can meander through this fate unharmed. I'm living, that's no choice, I didn't ask to be here. I didn't ask for this life, and I sure as hell never asked her to love me.

I didn't have a choice, no matter what she tells you, I didn't. She walked up all smiling and full of life. I didn't ask for no damn light, much less sunshine. I asked for peace, ordinary peace to help me to endure this life. Who the hell sent her? Why would they send HER to ME? You explain that, and then maybe I'll consider what it means to have a choice. I know you can't, I know I didn't choose her, she chose

me.

Chapter 2

If I told him the truth, he'd run and call me crazy. He would, there is not a doubt in my mind about that. He only wanted the sweet parts, the comfortable parts, so that's what I gave him. I had to. That's all he wanted. I tried to warn him that he'd get a stomachache from the sugar I'd bring to him, but he didn't believe me. Now he is bitter. He's angry because he doesn't know what to do next.

Choices? I giggle when I hear him ranting about that. Not because it is funny but because, he really believes that he has none. This Guy really thinks I walked up and did something strange to make him fall for me. He knows I'm from the south, so you know he had the nerve to ask me if I did voodoo on him! Imagine that!

Oh, he had a choice, he always did and no one could convince him otherwise. He wanted to be a victim. A victim of the good and the bad things that happened in his life. He's just so damn nonchalant, about EVERYTHING. You'd think he was sitting around waiting for the world to come tumbling down on him.

That's why he's mad about me. He's mad because he's been waiting for me to crumble. He does everything in his power to set me off, to shatter my happiness so I'll abandon him so he can go back to what he calls, "his ordinary life."

He doesn't even understand the blasphemy of his thoughts, he acts like I'm a GOD! I can't convince him that I have no power. I'm the witness for his life, just like he is for mine. But the truth is we both have choices over our own selves, and I choose to love him. But you can't convince him of that, he'll yell and tell you about the choices he had no control over, about how I made him do things he didn't want to do. I didn't, oh he chose…ask him, he chose….

Chapter 3

She said what? That girl has got you too. I can tell. Don't look at her for too long though or you'll have to see me, I don't care if you are a woman, she has this way that makes you forget who you are. You, you can't have her; don't try me. But anyway....

Ask my friends, my Aces.

They'll tell you.

I treated her like a trick, a bitch just like all the others. She was supposed to be another notch in the body count. I didn't choose her. She came to Me, all friendly and sweet. Looking and filling my senses like Carmel, the soft sticky kind that melts with too much heat. I intended to step into her presence, and give her this good stuff so I could tell everyone about how she was just like the others.

But she made me do something different, she wasn't normal, she WAS Carmel, but that stick to the roof of your mouth type, she sealed my lips shut and melted her goo all over my spirit, bonding me to her. She bonded with me, like that last bit of stickiness from a candy that is hard to wash off, I became a part of her somehow.

But didn't I say it was her?

She had me all covered in her being, now, you tell me how that was even possible for me to choose. She melted into me and I had NO say in that.

Hell, she had my friends looking at me all crazy, asking ME what my problem was.

You see my Aces and I had a bond. We moved against these Chicken-heads together. We traded stories and shared all the details of our newest additions to our lists. We were stacking bodies high. Like really, high with no regard for these hoe's feelings. I mean ladies, no regard for these ladies' feelings. She doesn't like it when I call women out of their names.

But, hell, none of the Crew has feelings, we are a unit, we all know the games women play and we understand it is necessary to get them before they get us. It is primal, the divine order, men rule over women.

So, true to our agendas of "get in and get out", I had one foot out. She had me looking at myself, which was no choice, I'm not the problem, I'm protecting myself. They are the problem. It was never about me before, why would it be now? It was always about THEM, those devious women, I had to stay ready with one foot out the door, and I stay ready.

Yes, I was ready when I met her. But she flipped it on me, not waiting for me to give her the goods; she acted like I had no say in the matter. I'd call her an Amazon but she was just too little to be that.

Of course, I wouldn't turn her down; Hell, I did try to, but she wasn't having it. I couldn't dare tell them about her, not when she was the one who gave in to me. I didn't have to give her false promises or lie to her about who I was. I didn't have to sell her anything, no stories, no fantasies; because she was uninterested, she didn't care one bit about any words I had to say.

Who does that?

Who just gives in?

She took away my plan, so tell me; how did I have a choice? My crutch was gone; I couldn't dare tell them that. We lie to these women but not to each other. My

Aces would know. She couldn't have the

upper hand on me. She's not like those

other women, and even though she is

dangerous, I mean she goes against the

grain. I couldn't step away from her either,

that woman had me curious.

But that is not a Choice.

It is not!

Chapter 4

I mean you have listened to him talk. It does not take a genius to understand that he was trying to rig the odds in his favor. It is not now, nor was it EVER about me.

He and his foolish ring of Aces are the problem. They sit and coax each other into believing that they do not need women. They share stories of conquering. They chant and laugh; hell, sometimes they even record and play pictures of the women to watch like an instant replay of a game. But if you were a fly on the wall you'd really realize that they are trading WAR stories.

They are out here treating love like it is War. But they are crazy because the only casualties are them! They are dead on the inside and they like being numb.

While they knock down bodies of women, they strengthen their belief that women are the problem. But I think it is sad. They are sad to me. They ARE choosing, he is choosing.

They choose damage.

Even a fool understands that if you are at WAR you don't consort with the enemy, for him, women are the enemy; that is why he blames me.

I am the choice, that held up a mirror to him. I made him see himself and he did not like that shit one bit. He had to look at scars and boy did he squirm when faced with that grotesque sight. Of course, he says he has no choice; he does not want to think he did this to himself. He cannot own up to it.

Chapter 5

War? See that's that craziness I'm talking about. She is always talking in puzzles. I'm not at War with women. I love women.

I never hurt them physically unless they were trying to hurt me. War means dead bodies, and I never killed anyone. Those women knew what was up. They understood the type of man I was and am. If she wanted to know anything, all she had to do was ask these streets. They know everything about you. That girl does not understand because she is not from these streets like me. She does not get it. War, that is laughable, she says the strangest things.

We are not talking about War we are talking about what she did to make me love her. Did she tell you that? Because I do not want to cat and mouse with her about what happened. I do not do this whole back and forth thing.

She knew I loved her. I did not have to keep telling her those things. That girl let me do what I wanted, right up until the day she tried to disappear from my life.

I couldn't understand, why didn't she stop Me? Why didn't she fuss? Why didn't she warn me?

I thought she had someone on the side, so I investigated her. I had them watching her, the streets you know, but they always fell in love with her. They would come back smiling. She would win them over without saying a word to them. They would report about how she smiled at everyone, or how she was generous with her time and energy; she did that shit to both males and females alike. They would get excited to tell me how helpful she was to people who really needed it. They made me tremble with fury; I wanted them to watch her, but not like that. After hearing them act a fool over her, they would always follow up with, "Yes, she was loyal."

A little part of me wanted to hear of her doing me wrong. Because then I could justify the suspicion I had, I mean this mistrust of her. No matter the report they gave, I would be indifferent to her. Nevertheless, she would still be passionate to ME.

The crazy part is while they were investigating her, they would always tell her something they should not have about me. They would say it was a slip. I'd go to her and she'd be all sad but somehow, still loving.

She would open the door, eyes puffy from crying, looking down at the floor; but she'd hug me so tight. That is when I knew.

LaShonda C. Henderson

Those were the only times I felt guilty; when she held me like that and not one tear fell from her face. She should have been crying, instead, her energy would be so heavy. Both of us would be walking in our heads, but sitting on the silence. We'd go to the movies to avoid addressing that heaviness. The only noise we'd make was to comment on whatever we were watching. The only time the silence would be broken is when I made love to her.

That was when she spoke.

She'd tell me she loved me and my heart would twitch a little bit and I'd kiss her to stop the words. Damn, why did she have to say those words then; because I would feel her open to me in that moment.

All that heaviness she held from first seeing my face, when she first opened the door, disappeared and all of a sudden, she would climax. You know what's crazy? She'd climax and I would be the one gasping for air, the room would be spinning, while I hung on to her for dear life.

War, hell no, we were not in a war. If anything, I was a hostage. She made me her hostage.

Chapter 6

He's right. I wouldn't cry. What the hell for? Tears don't move men. I never wanted to be that woman who used my tears as leverage, no; he didn't deserve to see them. I'm not stupid enough to think that his Aces told me things on accident. No. When I say they thought we were at War, I meant that!

They told me, so that I'd leave him, they wanted me to.

The thing about him is that he called me crazy. He really believed it too. I know that word could mean many things. I have never hurt him physically. I know you are wondering, so let me say it, no I never did any of those crazy things, you know those actions that carry the weight of those words. I didn't earn that label.

I know what you're thinking.

But just so we are clear, let me say it aloud. I've never followed him, never beat any girls up, never went through his phone, never showed up to his home unannounced, never disrespected his manhood in a public space. No, I was never that type of crazy. I just loved him. But I can tell you, from the way he treated me, that his definition of crazy could only mean a couple of things.

He has this thing about labels. He puts people in neat little categories. Let me tell you which one he put me in, so he could reason about having no choices.

He'd be quick to utter, "You are a smart woman" he'd throw it like a sword any time something became difficult between us. What I think he means, or rather, what I hear when he spews it out is, I am a woman that could do better. He means it. If you look into his eyes, when he talks about me, you'd understand the conflict that pours out of them; because to him, logic can't make me choose him, he is telling me that I am in a category of knowing better.

I kind of get it, his thought process I mean, he'd see a smart woman as the type to know how to acquire things. How to make people bend to her will, I tried to tell him, he is not a notch in my belt, not a hood ornament and definitely not one of those things to place on the shelf to be pulled out later. I knew what he meant by a Smart Woman, so to prove his point wrong, I chose to keep him a secret. If I was not flossing him around then I definitely couldn't be trying to keep him as an object of ownership. That had him stuck. He couldn't figure it out, why he could label me smart, but I act so contrary to his organized thought, so he removed that label and gave me a familiar universal woman category of being "crazy."

He had to call me that. I mean if I wasn't smart, then what was I? He couldn't put me in the category of not having my head on straight; there was just too much evidence against that. Crazy was a catch-all category, anything that didn't fit the norm fit neatly here. He and his Aces used it like a badge, hell they should have handed out pins so the women could keep up with our tag. They used it so frequently that it was disturbing.

Can't get her to sleep with them, she's crazy. She gives them her last dollar, she's crazy. Can't get her to chase them, she's crazy. She beats up any woman who is competition, she's crazy. Can't get her to conform, she's crazy. She sacrifices for them without being a wife, she's crazy.

It was easy to catch a label with that crew and his ass being the leader, was the standard setter. Of course he'd label me crazy, I mean I took his choices away; right, isn't that what he said?

Chapter 7

Hell Yea, she IS crazy, she is crazy as hell, now that is one thing she told you right. Crazy people leave you no choices. They walk into your life not listening. They don't care about any outcomes; they do what they want when they want. Have you tried fighting a crazy person? They'll kill you; you'll lose your life fucking with crazy people. Her, she is crazy smart, and I lost myself to her.

So back to choices, I didn't have one with her crazy ass.

Yea, she's right maybe they did tell her things on purpose, so she'd leave. Hell, I caught a couple of them whispering for her to leave me right in my face. My crew.

They wanted her to leave because those jokers had fallen for her, but they loved me too. They could see the train wreck we were. We were a pain waiting to happen in their eyes. They didn't want to see her upset, and they didn't want to see me broken; of course, they tried to shut us down. The two of us were a threat to our normal way of life, I choose my Aces without a bat of an eye, ain't no conflict about that, but her, I didn't choose. Label or no label, we just were.

Chapter 8

Finally, he begins to tell the truth. We just were. That is what he should be saying, what he said in those few words, he admits, that we were a choice. I'll bet you he sighed when he said it. I can see his face releasing the tension and all of that rage that builds with that word leaving him. We are getting somewhere.

So with this progress let me speak on MY choice.

I chose him.

I'm glad I did. He is everything I dreamed of and much of what I couldn't put into words. If I told you that, he is that biblical man that everyone dreams of you'd laugh. I know you would because you see how he talks and carries himself. But he is.

He is the type of man that we'd hear of in the bible. That convicted, sinner on the edge of change. Love is change and he didn't want to choose that. So I let him mold me.

Stop laughing.

I did. I let him mold me. I could tell you, before him, I was hell. I am the girl that fathers tell their sons to stay away from. Because he is right, I can make men do what I want. I am guilty of doing that over the span of my life. But him, no I chose to not be like that. I chose to let order move the both of us.

What do I mean by order?

I mean the natural flow of things, no one trying to rule over the other. Just being. But for that to work, choices MUST be made. I chose in every circumstance, every turn or decision, I went his way.

I wanted to let him lead. Not like, he does his Aces, no. I wanted to be led by that biblical part of him. That innate leadership that he was born with, I knew, if I had patience that he'd tap into it and I'd benefit.

I AM a smart woman, he was right to label me that, I am smart enough to recognize divinity when I see it. He reminded me of the story when God was walking among us, with Adam and Eve in the Garden, during the cool of the day, before the fall.

Chapter 9

See what I mean? Here she goes again. That girl knows she never went to church a day in adult life and here she is spewing that, "I saw God in him," speech.

All I am going to do is shake my head.

But what I can, say and mean, is that she is right about choosing me. She did. Over and over…mistake after mistake… she chose me when I know she should have left.

Hell, she almost did leave me once.

She messed up our rhythm with that. She had predictable behavior. Now that was something I love about her. I knew what she'd do. Normally, I'd do something wrong, avoid her for a while, then pop back up and love on her and she'd melt. But that one time, when I went to love on her, I couldn't get close to her. She threw me for a loop; it was in that moment I knew she was choosing me. I knew that at any moment she could and would take her choice back.

It was wild because I did some pretty vicious things to her. I cheated on her, I disrespected her in public, and I made her feel like she didn't matter to me. She did not budge in any of those moments. That is why I called her crazy. She had too much damn patience with me. However, that time, she left me; she stopped choosing me, for lying. Now here is the disturbing part, my actions never bothered her, but when she heard me tell a lie, an obvious one from my mouth, not from a text or an email but from my mouth, she left.

She went silent, her talkative ass went silent. I could hear the pain in her voice, when she tried to give me a moment to correct the lie, I knew that is what she wanted, but I did not stop the lie. I kept going. She responded by going too.

She shut off all access, my calls didn't make it through, I was no longer answered on the first ring, I didn't get responses from her in any format it, was like she shut down. I did not bump into her in our normal spots, I didn't see her face, I didn't see her smile, and I didn't get to hear her giggle. It felt like a dream.

I thought I would lose her I had to do something. I had to put the bullshit labels and suspicion away and I had to choose. So yea, I did choose. She made me. It was choosing her or be without her. I wanted her, she was ingrained in me, and I couldn't be without her.

Chapter 10

What does going to church have to do with me knowing God? He gets so wrapped up in the details of things.

But, Yea, I did almost give up on him. I really did. All that talk about him being from GOD went out the door when he lied to me. I can take many things. His actions, the things he did to keep his rep/street credibility did not bother me. So what, he said something smart to me in public, I'd never spark back at him, I'd just let him be. He flirted with women, took pictures with them and looked like the biggest pimp around. His Aces liked that, hell, he liked it. It made him proud. He likes to feel wanted.

But that lying to my face?

It was unacceptable. It made me lose control.

Let him live the life he wants. That is my motto. But I'll be damned if he thinks that I will let him be dishonest with me like he was with the world. No, I'm not having that, that is where I draw the line.

I cried by myself for days. Days! I had so much faith in him as a man. Before my eyes, his words took manhood away from him. I cried for him and for me. I let things be, and things took over him. He had to choose me because I gave up, I stopped choosing him.

Chapter 11

When she left me. When I thought I'd lost her. I could hear everyone talking about it. Just like my Aces thought, it broke her heart and it broke me. We were lost without each other. I missed her, I missed me with her, and how I felt when it was just us. She was my balance and I was uncoordinated, unable to hold on to anything; without her, I had no grip.

I overheard her friends defending her going ghost on me. They supported her leaving me with no hesitation. I heard them saying, with so much confidence, "Didn't ya'll watch him do what he wanted? They sounded all excited about what she'd do next. They were used to the old her, the one that would wreck your mind her. She was known for breaking egos. They wanted her to break me too.

They went on saying, "Pop your popcorn, she is going to live." I couldn't take it. I don't mean their words.

I couldn't take her silence.

They talked and she did and said NOTHING. I couldn't get close to her. Her friends went around saying, "The difference is, he hid his, but that girl is bold, she hides nothing. Let's see if your asses are still gleeful when she is done." They taunted my Aces, who were smirking about her disappearing.

Fuck all of them. Let the streets keep talking, for once I didn't care. I wanted her back. I needed her back. I wasn't me without her. I chose her. I wanted her, but I couldn't get close enough to tell her that. All I could think was where the HELL was she?

Chapter 12

Where did I go? Nowhere. I could not get out of bed. I wasn't hiding from him. I was hiding from me. I'm telling you it is easy to let men choose you. You do no work; if they go or you leave, it does nothing to you. But I chose him and for a second, for a minute, for days, I thought I was wrong.

I went inside of me. I turned to my mind. I felt like I was breaking without him. I was like that Caramel he talked about earlier, I was merged into him and to not choose him meant, not choosing me. I was lost. I was curled up in a little ball lost;

resting under my comforter, staring into nothing, but seeing everything. I was silent, because I didn't have words for what I felt. I walked around doing normal bodily functions, showering, brushing my hair into a bun, drinking water, going to relieve myself and getting right back into bed, into my ball.

I chose him and he chose himself. Therefore, I had to let go. I went through all of the scenarios where I trusted him and he must have lied. You see, when you look at the divinity of a person, you can't see the human part of him. I chose to make him a GOD to me, and I was being punished by his absence. You know, like my prayers were no longer being answered.

Now, my girls, they wanted to chant and boost me up to seek revenge on him. But I couldn't. You see, in choosing him the first time, I chose to change. Once you taste what freedom feels like, you won't go back to bondage. I love him. I knew I loved him and I didn't want to hurt him no matter how tight I had to curl up into this ball to be alright.

I left him. Mentally and physically and I went searching for ME.

Chapter 13

Damn.   Even now.   Hearing about where she was, her silence shakes me to the core. I know I said I didn't choose her when we started. I take it back. I did. I chose her over everything. That girl got into me. She touched my heart and moved me to choose happiness. She was a part of my happiness and I couldn't let her go.   She wasn't a showboat, she didn't boast about me and I mistook that, for her being embarrassed by me. But I get it now. She chose me.

Give me a minute.

I get what she was saying about me being divine to her.   She treated me like that. You could look at her and see her come alive when I walked into her space; like I had all the answers to the world in me. I knew she wanted me to lead her. I would from time to time but really, I was letting her lead me too.

Man, her laugh. That laugh made me guide her to open all those things she had hidden in her. It was like unwrapping a present. Each tare of paper, each ripping of ribbon, produced something so rare, a light so bright, so intense it made me feel crazy. However, I called her crazy instead. I chose her, to share with her, to let her be.

When I got her back. I showed her love that she had been asking for without words.   I made her pour love over me outside of the bedroom. But let me tell you. She was still silent from time to time; like she was remembering what she went through, where she went when I lied to her when she left me.

I chose her, I chose not to lie to her anymore and I choose to be ME.   That divine me that she sees in me.

Chapter 14

I choose him too. I chose to forgive him. He does many things I do not agree with.

But, If you ask my Momma, she'd tell you. I wasn't one of those daughters who talked incessantly about marriage. I didn't pull out bride books, I didn't talk about wedding rings or dresses, and I didn't plan anything.

If you ask her, she'd tell you, not many men crossed my lips. She thought I was a homosexual, because all she heard me talk about, were the women in my life. I didn't talk about committing to anyone. No one made my list beyond being a friend.

Ask her, she will tell you that I did not want to share my world with anyone. I only wanted GOD in my space. But if you ask her, she'll tell you; I love him, no matter what he does, even when I need to go silent for a while.

Go to heaven and ask her about my prayers to her, she will tell you about how I let go of my old way and how I merged with him. How my mind merged with his, how we sometimes say the same thing at the same time.

Genesis 2:24 states, "Therefore shall a man leave his Father and his Mother, and shall cleave unto his wife; and they shall become one flesh."

Yes, I chose him, but he chose me too. Don't ever forget. I believed in him, he believed in himself and we chose Each other.

Choices are life.

The End of the Myth

I lived in a glass house
One where people threw rocks
But they only cracked it
They weren't strong enough to break it
I lived in a glass house
One where everyone could see in
But they didn't know me
I lived in a glass house
One where you always knew when I was
home
But you didn't know if I was "there"
I lived...
Somehow, my voice shattered the walls...
I'm free
Sometimes I throw rocks back now
Sometimes I throw love back
But most of the time
I walk past where that house used to be
You know to remind me

You see, her story is what leads into

what true love is. No one defines it for you.

We learn to accept another person and their

flaws. Now, people may say she is mad or

crazy, but people love for different reasons. But really, we are all just reaching for the light that love gives. I don't condone cheating; I don't condone abusive language or behavior.

I do condone doing what works for you.

Some may call her story, a horror love tale. But I am sure there is more to her than just the words she graced our minds with. She tells what was most traumatizing and liberating to her. She talks about the outliers, the things that sparked thought in her own behavior.

Please remember the most important part, the message of her story, she tells you

how SHE dwells in Eden. That is her
Paradise. I know it seems such a sad story;
nonetheless, she comes to peace in a way,
few women would tolerate, but it is HER
peace.

I ask who are we to judge? Just as
we are individuals, our love is unique as
well. I cast no assumptions or throw no
rocks at her.

She sounds free....

But what do I know, I'm just an observer!

You can find
LaShonda on Facebook at

www.facebook.com/loveandotherthoughts

On
Instagram at
LoveAuthorLCH

On
The Net at
www.Cshantaypublishing.org